do you believe in Magic?

Samuel Boyd:
Thanks for
believing!
Olivia Millevoi

by Olivia Millevoi

illustrated by Stephen Marshall

The following story is based on true events.

"Matt, catch!" The football soared over the pavement still hot from the summer sun. The wind rustled the trees; their branches swayed, but their trunks remained steady, standing high above the boys who were playing. Great raindrops of many colors fell to the ground and landed on Magic, standing out on his dark fur, boldly. The ball landed on the curb...

Magic ran to it. It smelled leathery.

Matthew was right to it; he picked it up and threw it back to Alec. Magic rushed around their feet. Wind swept furiously through his fur. It felt like such a long time since he last ran. The boys had starting leaving him in the morning, with large sacks on their backs, only to come back later in the day, when the sun was less bright and the air was cooler.

The street got too hot; it pierced Magic's feet and he ran to the mushy grass. It tickled his belly as he lay to watch the football fly up into the air and down into the boys' arms again. He knew it would be cooler later on, and then he could go out again.

The next day, rain, not rain of bright colors, but dull, wet rain pattered against the window, destroying the view of the backyard. Magic reached out his tongue to clean his paw, a small pink ship in a sea of black. The boys had left him again. He did not know where they went every day, but he missed them and decided to make a softy pile to comfort himself.

Rio appeared at the doorway.
He jumped around Magic, barking loudly. He bathed his brother in kisses; his wet tongue made Magic's face sticky, like peanut butter. Rio then found a toy and excitedly pawed at it. Magic ran to the stairs to start his pile.

The laundry room was filled with machines that rumbled and bounced. Magic found a large basket in the corner of the room. He began to sniff the pieces, one by one. No, no, no...aha, yes! Magic took a silky blouse from the basket that smelled like mom and dragged it down into the living room.

Next he entered the open closet and dragged a coat that belonged to Nick on top of the blouse. What followed were some mittens of Alec's, a cap of Matt's, and a sheet that smelled like Dad. It was soon all piled up in the living room, and Magic laid on it for the rest of the day while watching Rio run around the coffee table. It was so soft, and it smelled so good, it was as if someone had placed a cloud right under him. He began to doze off...

The door slammed shut and Magic jerked his head up. Nick and Alec! They bent over and scratched Magic's back. "Look at what you did, you little shopper!" Nick said. He curved the edges of his mouth into a smile when he saw the pile. He did not let his tongue hang out. None of the two-legged people in the house ever did. Magic always thought this was strange, yet he licked Nick anyway. Rio tackled Alec, who nearly fell down.

Nick and Alec took out books and sat at the kitchen table. Mom arrived a while later with Matthew, who said hello to Magic and his brother. Rio seemed overwhelmed. Almost everyone was back! He barked and barked and barked like it was his last chance to bark again. "Look, our little shopper's been browsing the house again!" Mom reached down and patted Magic. He stood on the side of his pile proudly. He had created his own little work of art.

The next evening, when the two-legged members of the family left the house, it felt oddly cool. It was as if something strange was lingering in the air, waiting to pop out by surprise. Magic had spent the day napping on the couch, for it was another blank day when the boys were not home. Rio seemed to sense a weird feeling in the air too, because he spent most of the time lounging around on his bed. A minute may have passed, maybe a few, maybe a lot, and then it all happened in one second.

The air grew warmer. The heat beat on Magic's thick fur. Rio barked angrily and began to jump around, wanting to make it go away. Great puffs of grey emerged from the metal machine at the side of the kitchen. Magic was scared.

Suddenly, flickering creatures rose and took over the machine. Rio ran into the kitchen and continued to bark loudly. The creatures spread across the kitchen, multiplying. The smell of sizzling wood filled Magic's nostrils. It grew hotter!

Terrified of what would happen if the flaming creatures stayed any longer, Magic ran and stuck his head underneath the sofa and crouched low, shivering from fright. The creatures soon took over the whole kitchen, in shades much more fierce than autumn leaves.

And Magic waited.

Frightened and confused, he waited.

Finally, the garage door creaked open. Magic didn't make a sound. He felt someone pick him up and run him out of the house. Magic recognized the man's scent. It was Dad. The cold, wet grass touched Magic's feet as he was let down. It felt so refreshing after being so hot for so long! Above him, people's shouts boomed like cannons.

"What happened?" "Is everyone alright?" Magic did not understand their words. Mom was there. And Matt. Nick. Alec. Dad. A large man in a coat gave Magic a mask. The air that came out of it was clean and cool. Magic was not scared anymore. He jumped around people's feet. They continued to shout in confusion.

Smile at him. Cry.

Magic stayed outside for a long time. Where was Rio? He looked under bushes and around trees to see if his brother was there. He was not. Magic knew that it would be a long night.

Days later, Magic was in the car. Bump, bump, bump it went along. It stopped at a strange, unfamiliar house. It was not like home. It smelled different. The floors felt strange. It was near a busy street. Cars of different shapes and colors zoomed past every day. Magic would watch them go by in the afternoon. The boys continued to go out with backpacks.

Rio never returned.

Magic slowly got used to the new house. One day, Matt and Mom sat at the kitchen table.

"I've just thought of something," Mom said, putting her book down.

"What?" asked Matt.

"Don't you think it's funny that Magic knew what to do?"

"Knew what to do when?" Matt asked.

"During the fire! Magic stayed under the couch," Mom said.

They stayed quiet for a while.

"Mom!" said Matt suddenly.

"Mom, Magic! His name is Magic!"

Mom stared at him. Then she stared down at Magic. He wagged his tail.

"You're right," she said. The edges of her lips turned into a big smile. "His name is Magic."

He did not understand them, but he knew that they were happy. Looking down the hall, he wondered if he could make another softy pile.

He had nothing to lose.

He was Magic...

the dog who lived up to his name.

Author's Note

On the evening of September 18th, 2013, a fire broke out in the home of Allison, Bob, Nicholas, Alec, and Matthew Roda. The only witnesses to the starting of the fire were the family's two Labrador retrievers, Magic and Rio. Sadly, Rio perished that night due to smoke inhalation. Magic, however, somehow had an instinct to stay close to the ground and the instinct to survive. A portion of the proceeds from this book will be donated to families who have suffered as a result of house fires.

Magic continues to make softy piles.

Acknowledgments

In the three years since having written Magic's story, so many incredible people have helped me on the road to this final draft. My huge thanks to Dennis McNeill, retired firefighter, for teaching me about the nuances of fires and how they take form. To Michael DiFiori, graphic designer, for helping me with the layout of the story. To Steve Marshall, illustrator, for making each word come to life with his art. Your flexibility and talent are both amazing. To my family, friends, and Saint Andrew School teachers, for their encouragement and instruction.

And especially to Frank Murphy, children's book author; all of the dedication, honesty, time, and love you poured into helping me through this process will remain in my memory forever.

And to the Roda family, for sharing their story. This book is dedicated to you and your beloved dog, Rio.

35471306R00020

Made in the USA
Middletown, DE
04 October 2016